W9-AUQ-676

# The Case Of The

# ROCK & ROLL MYSTERY™

# The Case Of The
# ROCK & ROLL MYSTERY™

by Lisa Eisenberg

DUALSTAR PUBLICATIONS  PARACHUTE PRESS

SCHOLASTIC INC.

New York   Toronto   London   Auckland   Sydney

DUALSTAR PUBLICATIONS     ™     PARACHUTE PRESS

Dualstar Publications
c/o Thorne and Company
1801 Century Park East
Los Angeles, CA 90067

Parachute Press
156 Fifth Avenue
Suite 325
New York, NY 10010

Published by Scholastic Inc.

Copyright © 1998 Dualstar Entertainment Group, Inc. All rights reserved.
All photography copyright © 1998 Dualstar Entertainment Group, Inc.
All rights reserved.

The New Adventures of Mary-Kate & Ashley, The Adventures of Mary-Kate & Ashley,
Mary-Kate + Ashley's Fun Club, Clue and all logos, character names and other
distinctive likenesses thereof are the trademarks of Dualstar Entertainment Group, Inc.
All rights reserved.

With special thanks to Robert Thorne and Harold Weitzberg.

If you purchased this book without a cover, you should be aware that this book is
stolen property. It was reported as "unsold and destroyed" to the publisher, and
neither the author nor the publisher has received payment for this "stripped book."

No part of this publication may be reproduced in whole or in part, or stored in a
retrieval system, or transmitted in any form or by any means, electronic, mechanical,
photocopying, recording, or otherwise, without written permission of the publisher.

Printed in the U.S.A.
October 1998
ISBN: 0-439-04167-8
A B C D E F G H I J

# A CALL FROM
# A ROCK AND ROLL STAR!

"**Y**ou'll never believe what happened to me last night!" our friend Samantha cried. Samantha couldn't wait to tell me and my sister Ashley about the rock concert she went to last night.

And we couldn't wait to hear about it! The Bailey Brothers sang at the concert—and they're our favorite group!

"Tell us everything, Samantha!" I said. "Are the Bailey Brothers as cute as everyone says? What songs did they sing? Isn't it cool that

Bobby Bailey is nine years old like we are? Did he sing—"

"Mary-Kate!" Ashley interrupted me. "Slow down! You're not giving Sam a chance to talk."

Ashley and I are twins. But even though we look alike on the outside, we're totally different on the inside! For one thing, Ashley's always telling me to slow down. But sometimes that's really hard for me to do. I like to jump right into things—fast! Ashley likes to take her time.

Ashley and I are detectives. We run the Olsen and Olsen Mystery Agency out of the attic of our house in California.

That's where we were, in our house, sitting at our desks. Sam was sitting cross-legged on top of Ashley's desk.

And Clue, our basset hound, was lying at my feet. She was looking up at Sam. I think Clue was waiting to hear what happened at the rock concert, too!

I scratched Clue's long, floppy ears. Clue is

such a smart dog that Ashley and I made her a silent partner in our detective agency. Clue has a great nose for sniffing out clues!

"I know what happened," I joked to Sam. "Bobby Bailey sang a song just for you!" Bobby Bailey is the youngest member of the Bailey Brothers—and the cutest!

"I wish," Sam said in a dreamy voice. "I love him!" Sam laughed. Her brown eyes sparkled and her red curls bounced around her face.

"Well," Sam went on, "the Bailey Brothers were onstage and then...disaster struck!"

Ashley and I stared at Sam. "What went wrong?" we both asked at the same time.

*Rrrring!*

Ashley and I looked at each other. We really wanted to hear the rest of Sam's story. But whoever was calling might have a case for us!

I reached across my desk and picked up my blue telephone. Ashley picked up her pink telephone so she could listen in. "Olsen and Olsen Mystery Agency," I said. "Mary-Kate

Olsen speaking."

"My name is Theo Bailey," a boy's voice said. "I'm one of the Bailey Brothers."

My mouth dropped open. I covered the phone with my hand and whispered to Sam, "It's Theo Bailey!"

Sam's eyes opened really wide and she gasped.

"Are you one of the detective twins?" Theo asked.

"Yes, Theo," I told him. "And my sister Ashley is the other. She's listening in."

"I really need to hire you guys," Theo said.

I couldn't believe it! A rock star was calling us with a case! And Theo wasn't just any rock star! He was the oldest Bailey brother—sixteen, to be exact—and gorgeous!

"What's the problem, Theo?" Ashley asked.

"Someone is out to get my rock group!" he told us.

"What do you mean?" I asked.

"Someone set off about twenty stink bombs

during our first song two nights ago!" Theo told us. "The whole theater reeked of rotten eggs. The audience had to leave—holding their noses! Some people even fainted!"

Ashley and I both crinkled up our noses.

"And last night," Theo continued, "a stage light fell just as we were about to start singing. It could have really hurt us! We could tell that someone rigged it to fall."

"That does sound pretty weird," Ashley said.

"I think my brothers and I are in danger," Theo said. "Someone is definitely out to get us. But I don't know who. So we need your help before something *really* terrible happens. Please say you'll help—"

Theo didn't get to finish his sentence.

The phone line went dead!

# 2

## WE'RE GOING UNDERCOVER!

"**L**et's go!" I hung up the phone, jumped up from my desk chair and headed for the door.

"Not so fast, Mary-Kate," Ashley told me. "We don't even know where Theo was calling from. We can't just go rushing off."

"You have to do something!" Sam cried. "Theo might be hurt!"

"Maybe he just dropped the phone," Ashley began. "Or—"

*Rrring!*

I grabbed the phone. "Hello? Olsen and Olsen Mystery Agency." Ashley picked up her phone.

"It's Theo Bailey again," the voice on the phone said. "I heard somebody coming before. So I hung up and ran to a different phone. I can't let anyone know I'm hiring detectives."

"Why?" I asked.

"Because if whoever is doing this finds out that detectives are snooping around...you could both be in real danger, too."

Ashley and I looked at each other and gulped.

"If you take the case," Theo went on, "you'll have to go undercover."

Undercover—yes! I pumped my fist in the air. Investigating undercover means you can't let anyone know you're a detective. And that means you have to pretend to be someone else!

Ashley and I never investigated undercover before—but we've always wanted to. And here was our chance!

"You can pretend you're a rock band," Theo said. "That way, you can snoop around at the theater. And no one will suspect a thing! Can the two of you sing at all?"

Ashley and I stared at each other. "Well, we did sing a few songs at our school's talent show last fall," I said.

"That's good enough," Theo said. "Look, I'm desperate! I think my brothers will quit the band if things get worse. Kyle is so fed up he's *already* talking about quitting. And Bobby has his baseball team—he won't mind giving up the rock group."

We couldn't let the Bailey Brothers break up! They were our favorite group!

"We're supposed to go on tour in other cities," Theo said. "It's a big deal for us. But if my brothers quit—I really need your help. Will you take the case?"

I glanced at Ashley. She nodded.

"Theo, we'll take the case!" I told him.

Wow! This was the *double* chance of a lifetime!

The lead singer of our favorite rock band needed us!

And the Trenchcoat Twins were going undercover...as rock stars!

# CLUE'S FAVORITE CLUE

"**U**h-oh!" Ashley said as soon as we hung up the phone.

"What's wrong?" Sam and I asked Ashley at the same time.

"What are we going to do? Rock bands usually have a guitarist, a keyboard player, a drummer, *and* singers. Mary-Kate and I can't play all those instruments ourselves!"

"I'll help!" Sam offered. "Remember, I play the electric keyboard!"

"And I can play the electric guitar," I said.

"Ashley, you're great at shaking maracas to a beat."

Ashley took out her detective notebook from her jeans pocket and started writing down what we discussed so far.

"Okay," she said. "But we still need a drummer."

"Do we know any drummers?" I asked.

Ashley tapped her pencil on her notebook as we thought. Then we both let out a long, loud groan.

"What's wrong?" Sam asked.

"We do know a drummer," Ashley answered.

"And it's Princess Patty," I finished.

Now Sam groaned.

Princess Patty is our nickname for Patty O'Leary. She's in our fourth-grade class at school and lives next door to us. We call her Princess Patty because her parents buy her everything she wants and she acts so spoiled.

"I know she'll say yes if we ask her to be in

our group," Ashley said.

"And we all know she'll want to be the star of the show," I muttered.

"She'll complain all the time," Ashley added. "But she *was* pretty good on drums at the talent show."

"Okay. We'll call her later." I sighed.

"Hey!" Ashley said. "What about a name for our group?"

"I know!" Sam said. "How about Twin Trouble! It's a great name for twin lead singers."

Ashley and I grinned. "Great idea, Sam!" I told her, and gave her a high five. "Twin Trouble, here we come!"

It was two hours later, and our rock group was pedaling down the street. Clue sat in the basket of my bike. Ashley's basket held our outfits. And Patty's basket overflowed with cans of hair spray!

Before we left, we had one quick rehearsal

in the garage. Then Theo called again. He told us he had talked to the rock concert manager about us. He told her we would be investigating the case undercover as a rock band. Our mom had already dropped off our instruments at the theater. Everything was set!

"I still don't see why we have to ride bikes to the rock concert," Patty whined. "My helmet is messing up my hair."

I looked over at Patty and groaned to myself. "Patty, the theater is only a ten-minute ride from our houses," I explained for the third time. "We need our bikes so we can come and go quickly while we're investigating."

"Whatever!" Patty said. "But when we get booed off the stage because the drummer has messy hair..."

We'd been a rock group for only two hours, and Patty was already complaining about everything.

We pedaled into the theater parking lot and locked up our bikes. I helped Clue out of the basket and we all raced inside. We headed down a long aisle toward the stage.

"I just wanna be your friend!" we heard a boy's voice sing out.

The Bailey Brothers! I could see the three boys standing under a spotlight on the stage. This was so exciting!

The tallest one was Theo. Next to him was Kyle. Kyle was really cute too. He was twelve and had light brown hair and green eyes. And next to Kyle was...Bobby—right in front of our eyes!

Bobby had curly blond hair and dark blue eyes. He was wearing a baseball uniform and baseball cleats. He must have come from baseball practice, I thought. Bobby Bailey was multi-talented!

I started bopping to the beat of their music. So did Sam. I even started to sing along. Then I felt a nudge in my ribs.

"Shh!" Ashley whispered. "They're rehearsing. We have to be quiet."

"Okay, okay," I whispered back. "Let's get closer!"

We all tiptoed down the aisle toward the stage. We climbed the four stairs that led up to the side of the stage.

*Thwump!*

"What was that horrible sound?" I asked.

"It sounds like an electric bass," Sam said. "But there's something *really* wrong with it."

Theo was staring at his guitar. "Hey! *Someone* stuffed a towel in my bass!" he yelled.

Suddenly, Clue barked and ran over to Theo. She started sniffing the bass like crazy!

"Oops," I said. I ran out onto the stage. "Here, Clue."

But Clue was pulling something out of the bass. It wasn't a towel after all. It was a long white and blue tube sock. Clue ran toward backstage with it in her mouth.

"That might be a clue!" Ashley whispered in my ear.

We ran across the stage. "Clue! Clue! Come back here!"

Clue disappeared around a corner. Ashley and I raced after her.

And then we crashed right into someone.

"Owwwwwwwww!" a boy yelped.

The boy was dressed in black from head to toe with white stars stitched all over his clothes.

"Hey! Watch where you're going!" he yelled.

"Sorry! We—" But the boy interrupted me before I could finish my sentence.

"Figures!" he shouted as he looked toward the stage. "Those stupid Bailey Brothers are holding up rehearsal *again*. I hate them! I wish they would disappear!"

My mouth dropped open.

We had our first suspect!

## 4

# SIMON SAYS

"**W**hat are you two doing back here?" the boy growled at us. "Only rock groups are allowed backstage."

"We *are* a rock group," Ashley explained. "A new one called Twin Trouble."

"We've just joined the concert," I added.

"Who are you?" Ashley asked.

"I'm Simon," the boy said. "I'm the lead singer of Simon and the Shooting Stars."

"Is that a rock group?" I asked.

"No, it's a rock slide!" Simon snickered in a

mean voice. "Of *course* it's a rock group. We're in the rock concert, too."

Clue trotted back to us and lay down at my feet. She chewed on the sock she pulled out of Theo's bass.

"That sock stinks!" Simon said, holding his nose. He bent down and tried to pull the sock out of Clue's mouth. But Clue jumped up and ran off with it.

Good girl! I knew our dog would never give a clue to anyone but Ashley or me. That's one of the things that makes her such a great silent partner.

I really wanted to get that sock from Clue. I had to put it in my evidence bag. But I also wanted to talk to our first suspect!

Simon glared at the Bailey Brothers onstage. "Well, Twin Trouble, welcome to the worst rock concert in the world," he said to us.

"Why is it the worst rock concert?" I asked.

I wish I could take out my mini tape

recorder to interview Simon! I thought. But I can't, I reminded myself. I'm undercover!

"It's the worst rock concert in the world because of those idiots out there." Simon pointed to the stage.

"Idiots?" Ashley asked. "You mean the Bailey Brothers?"

"No! I mean the Bailey *bozos*!" Simon groaned. "Those Bailey bozos get treated like big stars. It's disgusting," he added.

"What do you mean?" I asked.

"Just wait till you get onstage. No one will listen to you sing. Everyone comes only to see the Bailey bozos! That's because the concert manager sends pictures of only *them* to the newspapers—and never pictures of us!"

Simon sneered and walked away.

"Ashley," I whispered, squeezing her hand. "I think we've solved the case!"

Ashley's big blue eyes opened even bigger. "What are you talking about?"

"It's Simon!" I said. "Don't you see? He

hates the Bailey Brothers! We heard him say he wanted them to disappear. He wants his band to get all the attention. Simon's definitely the culprit!"

Ashley looked to the left and then to the right. When she was sure we weren't being watched, she took out her notebook from her pocket.

"He's definitely a suspect," Ashley said. She wrote down Simon's name under *SUSPECTS*. "But we can't be sure he's the culprit, Mary-Kate. We just started investigating."

"But Simon sounded so angry," I said. "And—"

I didn't finish my sentence. That's because I suddenly heard a *very* familiar voice coming from around the corner.

"Ha!" the voice was saying. "I don't believe that for a minute!"

The voice belonged to Princess Patty. And it sounded as if she were doing some investigating herself!

"Who's she talking to?" Ashley asked.

"Let's go find out!" I said.

Ashley and I tiptoed around the corner. The area behind the stage was dark. But we could see Princess Patty and two boys. The boys looked about our age. One had red hair and freckles. The other had curly brown hair. They were both wearing off-white baseball uniforms and baseball cleats like Bobby Bailey's.

"So, you say you can't remember where you were when the stink bombs went off the other night!" Patty said to the boys.

Oh no! Patty *was* investigating! She was going to blow our cover!

"And you say you're *allowed* backstage— even though you're not a rock band?" Patty went on. "Ha! I think—"

Ashley and I rushed over to them. "Hi, Patty," I interrupted her. I gave her a look that told her she'd better be quiet!

"Hi!" I said to the boys. "I'm Mary-Kate, and this is my sister Ashley. We're part of a new rock band called Twin Trouble."

"Hi," the boy with the red hair said. "I'm Daryl and this is Jack. We're friends of Bobby Bailey. We're on the same baseball team."

"Yeah, and Theo told us we could hang out backstage and watch the bands rehearse," Jack explained.

"Let's go find Bobby," Daryl said to Jack. "See you later," he added to us.

The boys walked away.

Ashley frowned at Patty. "Why were you questioning Bobby Bailey's friends?" she asked. "Mary-Kate and I are *undercover*, Patty!"

"So?" Patty said, studying her light blue nail polish.

"So we're not supposed to be obvious!" I said. "We have to be careful about how we get information. No one is supposed to find out detectives are on this case!"

"So I can talk to whoever I want! *I'm* not a detective!" Patty said.

"That's right—you're *not*!" I pointed out. "And if you blow our cover, we could be in danger!"

Patty stuck her nose into the air. She turned and marched off toward the dressing room.

"Mary-Kate!" Ashley whispered in my ear. "I hear people arguing."

We stood still, trying to figure out where the voices were coming from.

"I think whoever is arguing is around this corner," Ashley said.

We both held on to the wall and peeked our faces around the corner. It was dark. But I could see three shadowy figures huddled together about ten feet away from us.

"Let's go listen!" I whispered. "They might be saying something important." I pulled my mini tape recorder out of my pocket.

"I'd better stick around here and keep an eye on Patty," Ashley said.

"This is such a pain! If only we didn't need a drummer," I muttered.

"Be careful, Mary-Kate!" Ashley warned.

I nodded and crept around the corner. It was really dark! I hugged the wall as I tiptoed farther down the hall. The arguing was louder now. It sounded like...Theo Bailey yelling at someone!

I couldn't hear everything he was saying. I tiptoed a few steps closer. I spotted a shadowy corner to hide in and crept over to it. I turned on my tape recorder and crouched down to listen.

"Kyle...ruining everything!" I heard Theo say.

"...not the end of it...be sorry!" Kyle shouted back.

"...lots of problems!...stop yelling!" That was Bobby Bailey's voice.

"...and you...ruining everything!"

*Ruining everything*, I repeated to myself. Was Theo talking to Bobby? Or Kyle? Did he think one of his *own brothers* was out to get their group?

I have to move closer, I thought. I need to hear everything.

With my tape recorder clutched in one fist, I got down on my hands and knees.

I started to inch forward on my stomach. But I froze when I heard a noise.

Breathing.

Someone was breathing right next to me!

# PRINCESS PATTY
# GETS CROWNED

Suddenly, something wet and warm touched my cheek.

*Snuffle. Snuffle. Snort. Snort.*

"Clue!" I whispered. "It was you!"

Clue still held the sock in her mouth. I reached for it but stopped when I heard Ashley call me.

"Mary-Kate! Where are you?" she whispered.

"Over here, Ashley!" I called back.

"It was the Bailey Brothers arguing!" I told

Ashley as she crouched down next to me.

"What were they saying?" she asked.

"I couldn't hear everything," I said. "But it sounded like Theo was telling Kyle that Kyle was ruining everything!"

"Wow!" Ashley said.

"Do you think Kyle could be a suspect?" I asked.

"Well, we should add him to our list," Ashley said. "But I hope we can cross him off as we investigate."

I knew what Ashley meant. It would be awful if one of the Bailey Brothers were out to get his own group!

The Bailey Brothers left the hallway. Then we left, too, and checked the theater from top to bottom. Sam and Patty said they wanted to watch the bands rehearse. Clue was baby-sitting our first clue for us—the sock—but she wouldn't let go of it. So far we hadn't found any more clues.

"Yoo-hoo!" A woman with a clipboard ran

down the hall toward me and Ashley. "Mary-Kate? Ashley?"

"That's us!" I told the woman.

"I'm Annette Sorenson, the concert manager," she said. "You girls had better get changed! Twin Trouble goes on in a half hour!"

The woman checked her clipboard. "Yup. You're on right after the Bailey Brothers. They go on in ten minutes. I met your friends Sam and Patty—they're in your dressing room."

"Thanks, Annette," I said.

We hurried to the dressing rooms. We opened the door just as Sam was coming out.

"You look so great!" I told her. She was wearing a short, shiny red jacket and a black miniskirt. Sam grinned and left to check on our instruments.

"And what about me?"

Princess Patty pranced around the room. She was wearing a long purple satin gown. Something sparkled on top of her head.

"Oh, no," Ashley groaned when she saw it.

"You're wearing a crown?" she shrieked.

"Patty!" I said. "What happened to the outfits we agreed on?"

"I prefer this one," Patty said. She tossed her head and marched off toward the stage.

Ashley and I stared at each other. Then Ashley looked at her watch. "We can't do anything about Princess Patty now," she said.

"Hey! What are you two doing in here? These dressing rooms are for rock groups only!" A tall blond girl stomped into our dressing room and yelled at us. She was wearing a long, sleeveless white dress. Her eyelids, cheeks, and arms were covered with bright green glitter.

"We *are* a rock group," I told her. "A new one called Twin Trouble."

The girl stepped right up to us. She planted her hands on her hips. "You're Twin Trouble, all right!" She smiled a nasty smile. "*Trenchcoat* Twin Trouble!"

**6**

# COVER BLOWN!

"**O**h, no!" I whispered to Ashley. "She knows we're detectives! Our cover is blown!"

The girl looked us up and down. "I've seen you two snooping around all afternoon," she said. "I thought there was something familiar about you. And then I remembered! I saw you two in a magazine. You're those detectives!"

I glanced at Ashley. I could tell she was thinking—hard!

"We used to be detectives," Ashley told the blond girl. "But we're rock singers now."

The girl's eyes narrowed. "Oh, really! I'm going to ask Annette Sorenson if that's true."

Oh, no! I thought. The girl can't ask anyone questions about us! Whoever we're after might overhear—and get suspicious of me and Ashley. That could put us in real danger!

I had to stall the glitter girl until we could think of a plan.

"Hey," I said to her. "How does all that glitter stick on your arms?"

"Duh! I spray hair spray on my arms," she said. "That makes the glitter stick. As Heather Lewis, president of the Glitter Fan Club, I—"

I had to interrupt her. "Um—there's a fan club for glitter?"

Heather rolled her eyes. "Not *this* stuff!" she said, pointing to the green glitter on her arm. "I mean Glitter, the rock group. They're the best group in the concert."

"The only group we know is the Bailey Brothers," I said.

Heather put her hands on her hips and

frowned. "Those jerks! They get to sing twice as many songs as the Glitter girls do."

I looked at Ashley. I could tell she was thinking exactly what I was! Heather was Suspect #3!

Heather glanced up and down the hallway. "I'm going to find Annette so I can ask her if you're *really* rock singers."

"Hey! I love your hair." Patty said, strolling into the room. "And that glitter is really cool."

"Your crown's cool, too," Heather said.

I had an idea! "You know," I said quickly. "You two would love that new shop that just opened around the corner from here."

"A new shop?" Patty and Heather squealed together.

"It's awesome!" I gushed. "It has great clothes, earrings, hair bands, back packs—"

"Patty," Ashley said with a big smile. "You have about twenty minutes to check out that shop. Why don't you and Heather go. But be back here in exactly twenty minutes! That's when our act goes on."

Patty and Heather didn't waste a second. "Let's go!" they both shrieked, and headed for the exit.

"Whew!" I said to Ashley the instant they were gone. "That was close!"

"Well, we've managed to keep Heather from asking questions about us—at least for twenty minutes," Ashley replied.

"The Trenchcoat Twins must be even more famous than we thought!" I said. "Heather recognized us really fast."

"I know! The next time we go undercover, real disguises are a must!" Ashley said.

Ashley slipped her notebook out of her jeans pocket. "Before I get changed, I want to add our two new suspects to our list," she said. I watched her add the names Kyle and Heather under *SUSPECTS*.

"But what are their motives?" I asked.

Our great-grandma Olive taught us what a motive is. It means a person's reason for doing something. Great-grandma Olive loves mysteries. She told us so many great detective stories that Ashley and I decided to become detectives ourselves.

Next Ashley wrote *MOTIVE* in the notebook. "Okay. Let's start with Kyle. Why would he want to ruin the Bailey Brothers?"

"I'm not sure," I said, frowning.

"Me either," Ashley said. "Let's skip to Simon and Heather. Suspect #1: Simon—he said he hates the Bailey Brothers!"

"Right," I agreed. "Because the Bailey Brothers get more attention than Simon and the Shooting Stars!"

*Knock-knock-knock!*

Someone was pounding on the door!

"Mary-Kate! Ashley! Are you in there?" It was Annette.

I jumped up and opened the door.

Annette looked really upset.

"Something horrible has happened!" she cried. "The Bailey Brothers are missing!"

# WE'RE ROCK AND ROLLERS

"**M**issing!" Ashley and I yelped together. "Are you sure?"

"Yes! They left right after rehearsal. And they haven't been back since!"

"Did you call their house?" Ashley asked.

"Yes! Five times! There's no answer! What am I going to do? They're supposed to go on in a few minutes! And they're the main act of the concert!"

Annette looked at her watch. "Well, you'd better get changed in a jiffy! Twin Trouble will have to go on first instead of the Bailey Brothers! I saw Sam by the side of the stage. But I haven't seen Patty."

"Um, speaking of Patty—" I was about to tell Annette that we just sent our drummer shopping!

Annette interrupted me. "Hurry! Hurry! You have to go on now! The Bailey Brothers will probably show up by the time you're done with your songs!" Then she rushed off.

"Do you think the Bailey Brothers are okay?" I asked Ashley. "Where do you think they could be?"

"I don't know." Ashley looked worried. "But we have to go onstage now. Maybe Annette's right. Maybe they'll be back by the time we're done."

We weren't expecting Patty back for at least fifteen minutes. Which meant that Twin Trouble was about to make its debut without their drummer!

Ashley and I pulled on our outfits. We were

both wearing black miniskirts and sparkly V-necked T-shirts. Plus, we both had on short, shiny jackets, black tights, and black ankle boots. The only difference was that Ashley's jacket was purple. Mine was blue.

"Wow!" I said, checking us out in the mirror. We brushed our hair and put on our matching black headbands. "We really do look like rock stars!"

"Let's just hope we *sound* like rock stars without a drummer!" Ashley said.

*Pound-pound-pound!* Another knock on the door.

"Who could that be?" Ashley asked.

"Maybe it's Annette!" I cried. "To tell us the Bailey Brothers came back!"

I yanked open the door. It wasn't Annette.

Simon stood there glaring at me and Ashley.

"Why does *your* group get to go on first?" Simon yelled. "Twin Trouble is new to the concert! Simon and the Shooting Stars should go on first! It's not fair!"

"Annette told us we were on—" I said, but Simon interrupted me.

"My group is the best act in the concert!" he shouted. "We're the only ones who sing *and* dance." He lifted his foot and showed us the bottom of his pointy black shoe. We could see little steel taps attached to the toe and heel.

"Your dumb group probably doesn't dance either, right!" Simon demanded.

"We just sing, but—" Ashley told him.

"So *we* should be on stage—and not *you*!" Simon interrupted her. "I'm going to find Annette right now—"

"And now I'd like to introduce a new local group," we heard Annette say onstage. "Let's hear it for Twin Trouble!"

"Sorry, Simon, but I guess we're on!" I told him. "Let's go, Ashley!"

I couldn't help but feel bad for Simon. After all, we weren't even a real rock group—and we still got to go on before his act!

But Ashley and I couldn't think about Simon now. We were about to go onstage—in front of a lot of people!

"Look, there's Sam!" Ashley said as we raced down the hall toward the stage.

We all ran onstage and took our spots.

Wow! There were a lot of people sitting in rows and rows of seats!

Yikes! What if we sounded awful without our drummer?

What if we sounded awful even *with* our drummer?

What if—

*Clack-clack-clack!*

What was that? It sounded like footsteps— but *weird* footsteps.

"Do you hear it?" I whispered to Ashley.

"Yes," she whispered back.

*Clack-clack-clack!*

Ashley looked around to see where the sound was coming from. Then she glanced up.

"Oh, no!" she whispered.

I tilted my head and looked up. Ulp!

Someone was up there. In the rafters right over the stage. I saw a flash of white move really fast.

Right over our heads.

"I'll bet it's the person we're after!" I said to Ashley.

"What's he doing?" she asked.

"I can't see him anymore," I told her. "We have to go up there and investigate!"

"We can't, Mary-Kate! We have to start singing!"

She was right!

I looked up again, but I didn't see anyone. Okay, I told myself. Open your mouth and sing!

I opened my mouth. I started singing.

The audience clapped along to our song. They liked us!

This was fun! I started bopping to the beat. Right in the middle of my twirl I saw Patty run out onto the stage and sit behind her drums.

Wow! I was actually thrilled to see Patty!

Then, *SPLASH*!

All of a sudden, a ton of cold water poured down on my head. I was drenched!

We all stopped playing as the water gushed everywhere.

I whirled around. Ashley, Sam, and Patty were soaking wet too!

"Waaaaaaaaaaah! My hair is ruined!" Princess Patty cried. For once I thought Patty had a right to complain!

The water kept raining down on us.

"Where is all this water coming from?" Sam yelled.

*Clack-clack-clack!*

"Ashley! Do you hear that?" I gazed up at the rafters.

Ashley tilted her dripping head and listened hard. "The *clack-clack-clack* footsteps," she cried. "Whoever drenched us is getting away!"

"Now's our chance to get him!" I cried.

# 8

# CLACK-CLACK-CLACK!

Ashley and I raced through the puddles of water. We hurried up the ladder that led to the rafters.

When I reached the top, I saw where the water was coming from—water sprinklers! They're supposed to go on only if there's a fire onstage. But someone turned them on so we'd get drenched! Or *worse*! We could have gotten really hurt. Electric instruments— electric *anything*—should never get wet. It's a major safety hazard!

I pulled my penlight out of my pocket and shone it around the rafters. I found the sprinkler knob and turned the water off.

I crawled around, searching the rafters for clues. "Did you find anything?" Ashley asked as she climbed up beside me.

"Not yet," I said. I brushed wet hair out of my eyes. "Did you catch him?"

"No," she said. "Whoever it was got away!"

She pulled her little notebook and flashlight out of her pocket. She made a new heading called CLUES. Under it, she wrote "*clack-clack-clack* footsteps."

"What kind of shoes would make a funny sound like that?" she asked.

"Let's see," I said. "Tap shoes like Simon wears? High heels like Heather's?"

"That doesn't help. I guess lots of shoes could make a *clack-clack-clack* sound." Ashley sighed. "What other clues do we have so far?"

"The white blur," I said. "I saw something white right before the sprinklers came on."

Ashley wrote that down. "Anything else?"

"What about this?" I cried. I pointed to something shiny on the rafter next to me. "It's green glitter! Just like Heather has on her arms!"

Ashley shone her flashlight on the glitter. "You're right!" she said. "Let's collect some of it and see if it matches Heather's!"

I took out our plastic evidence bag from my pocket. Then I used my fingers to carefully scrape some of the glitter into it. Ashley wrote "glitter on rafters" under the *CLUES* heading.

"If it's Heather's glitter, that proves she was up here!" I said. "She's who we're after!"

"Maybe," Ashley said. "But something about the timing bothers me. Heather was out shopping with Patty. And we know Patty came back right before the sprinklers went on. So Heather had only a minute or two to climb up here and turn on the sprinklers."

"But maybe Heather came back early!"

"That's what we have to find out!" she

replied. "I know—I'll talk to Patty about exactly when they came back. And you talk to Heather."

"And then we'll meet up and compare notes on what they say." Ashley said. She closed her notebook and put it back into her pocket with the evidence bag.

We climbed down the steps. When we reached the bottom, we saw two men in janitor's suits mopping up the wet stage.

I had a feeling I knew where a soaking wet Princess Patty would be. In the dressing room—fixing her hair.

I was right. I found Patty blow drying her hair.

"My crown will never be the same after getting all wet! My father will just have to buy me a new one," Princess Patty whined.

I rolled my eyes. "Never mind that now," I said. I pulled out my mini tape recorder and turned it on. "I have to ask you some questions about Heather. You and Heather went shopping—"

"*Tried* to go shopping," Patty interrupted.

".What do you mean, tried?"

"We went to the shop, but it was closed," Patty explained.

"So, since it was closed, did you come right back to the theater?" I asked.

"No—we looked in the shop's window. I was so mad that it was closed. I saw some really cool stuff in the window. Heather and I have the same great taste in clothes and—"

I groaned to myself. Princess Patty was so... so...princessy! "Patty, did you and Heather come back to the theater at the same time?"

"Yes," Patty replied.

"Was Heather with you every single minute until you came on stage with us?"

"Let me think," Patty said. "We got back to the theater. Heather told me again what great nail polish I had on—"

"Patty! Stick to the facts, please!"

"All right, all right! So Heather saw that you

were on stage, and she got really mad. She said Glitter should be on instead."

My eyes opened wide. "Then what happened?"

"I ran onstage and sat behind my drums," Patty said. "I don't know what Heather did after that."

The dressing room suddenly banged open.

It was Heather.

"I have a note for you, Mary-Kate," Heather said. "It's from your nosy sister Ashley. You know what? She just asked me a lot of questions—for an *ex*-detective."

Heather handed me the note. "Hey, wait a minute," she said, frowning. "It's blank. Why would Ashley ask me to give you a blank piece of paper?"

Heather put her hands on her hips and glared at me. "Well, Miss I'm-Not-A-Detective-Anymore!" she said. "I'm waiting for an answer!"

## WHERE ARE THE BAILEY BROTHERS?

**G**ood question! I thought, frowning.

Why *would* Ashley give Heather a blank piece of paper to give to me?

Then it hit me!

Ashley wrote me a note using invisible ink! That way, no one could read the note but me!

"Um, maybe she handed you the wrong piece of paper or something, Heather," I explained quickly. "I'll go find her."

What I was *really* going to find was a hair dryer—in another dressing room.

I ran to the dressing room down the hall

and found a hair dryer. I turned it on to the lowest setting. Then I held the note in front of the heat and waited.

I had a feeling that Ashley had written the note with a paintbrush dipped in milk. That's why it was invisible!

Sure enough, the heat from the hair dryer turned the milk message brown. The invisible milk ink became visible! I read Ashley's note:

*Heather claims she watched our song and washout from the side of the stage. She also says somebody stole all her glitter!*

*Meet me in the little park down the block ASAP. We can talk in private there!—Ashley*

ASAP stood for "as soon as possible." I ran out of the building and headed for the park. I spotted Ashley sitting on a bench. Her detective notebook was open on her lap.

"Okay," she said as I sat down next to her. "Let's go over what we know so far."

Ashley slipped the little evidence bag out of her pocket. "I took a really good look at the glitter on Heather's arms," she said. "It matches what we found on the rafters."

"So it's definitely her glitter. That proves she was up there! Oh—wait a minute," I added. "Heather told you that someone *stole* her glitter. But we don't know if she's lying!"

"Right!" Ashley agreed.

"And she's definitely on to us," I told Ashley. "She knows we're still detectives."

"I guess we can't worry about that now," Ashley said.

"Okay. Let's talk about Suspects #1 and #2. Simon and Kyle Bailey. We should find out where they were when the sprinklers went on."

"Good idea." Ashley made a note of that in her notebook. "Wait a minute! Kyle Bailey can't be a suspect!"

All of a sudden I knew what Ashley meant. "Because Kyle wasn't even in the theater when the sprinklers went on! Ashley, the Bailey Brothers are missing! We forgot to see if they made it back to the concert!"

Ashley and I jumped up from the bench and ran back to the theater.

"Mary-Kate," Ashley stopped and grabbed my shoulders. "I just thought of something really bad!"

"What?" I asked.

"The stink bombs, the stage light falling, the sock in Theo's bass—all those mean things happened to the Bailey Brothers."

"And?" I asked.

"The sprinklers went on when *we* were on stage! Whoever is out to get the Bailey Brothers is out to get *us*, too!" Ashley said.

"Theo told us we could be in danger if the bad guy found out detectives were investigating. I bet it *is* Heather!"

"Maybe," Ashley said as we rushed into the theater.

We found Annette pacing back and forth in the hallway. Clue was pacing with Annette. She still had that sock in her mouth!

I could hear Glitter onstage. Simon and his band members were waiting by the side of the stage to go on next.

I was about to take the sock from Clue when Annette ran up to us. "No one knows where the Bailey Brothers are!" Annette cried. "They've disappeared!"

"Let's check their house!" I said to Ashley. "Annette, do you have their address?"

"123 Upland Drive!" Annette said. "It's very close to here."

Ashley, Clue, and I raced to the parking lot. Ashley and I put on our helmets, jumped on our bikes and pedaled away. Clue sat in my bike's basket. The wind whipped Clue's fur around as we rode.

"Here it is!" I yelled after we'd ridden a few blocks. "It's that big gray house just up ahead."

"Hey! Look!" Ashley shouted. "That car is backing out of the Baileys' driveway!"

We watched a brown and white mini-van shoot out of the driveway really fast. Gravel spewed up into the air in all directions.

The car screeched out onto the street. As it sped away, I tried to see who was inside. I couldn't see who was driving. But I could see a boy with curly blond hair in the backseat of the mini-van.

"Ashley!" I cried. "That was Bobby Bailey in the backseat. He's being kidnapped!"

# THE SHOW STOPPER!

"After them," I yelled. "Someone's kidnapping Bobby Bailey!"

"We can't keep up with a car!" Ashley shouted back as we pedaled as fast as we could. "It's getting away!"

"Let's try to memorize the license plate! Can you see what it is?" I asked.

"Yes! It says I-H-V 8-2-2!"

"I-H-V 8-2-2," I repeated. How can I remember that? I wondered. I-H-V sounds sort of like 'I have.' And eight sounds like 'ate.' And two

two could be 'too too.' That's it! 'I have ate too too much.'

"The police station is just around the corner," Ashley said, pointing at the street sign. "Maybe Inspector Williams can check who the license plate number belongs to."

"Good idea!" We turned the corner. We got off our bikes and chained them to a bike rack in the station parking lot.

We were in luck. Our friend Inspector Williams was just coming out the station door. He's helped us out on a lot of our cases.

"We think a friend might be in trouble. Can you help us?" Ashley asked. "Can you trace the license plate of a car right away?"

"No problem," Inspector Williams said. "Nothing's too much trouble for the Trenchcoat Twins." He bent down to pat Clue on the head. "Hey! What's Clue chewing on?" he asked as we all hurried into the building. Clue trotted beside us.

"Clue's baby-sitting a clue for us!" I said.

The inspector laughed. "Now, what was the number you needed?" he asked us.

"Um," said Ashley, "what was it, Mary-Kate?"

"I have ate too too much!" I said.

Everyone stared at me. My face turned red. Then I said, "I mean, I-H-V 8-2-2."

The inspector laughed again and tapped out the letters and numbers on his computer keyboard. "Let's see," he said. "That license plate is registered to a Mr. Theodore Bailey at 123 Upland Drive."

Ashley and I stared at each other. "Theodore Bailey?" Ashley repeated. "Do you think that's Theo?"

"Or maybe it's the Bailey Brothers' father," I said. "Either way, Bobby Bailey was in his own family's car when we saw him."

Ashley breathed a sigh of relief. "Wow, am I ever glad to hear that. Bobby probably wasn't kidnapped after all. But we have to make absolutely sure."

"Well, where do you think they were going?"

"Maybe to the theater!" Ashley suggested.

"Let's check it out!" I exclaimed. "Thanks, Inspector Williams," I said. "Come on, Clue!"

We left the building, climbed onto our bikes, and pedaled as hard as we could back to the theater.

It started to rain lightly just as we pulled into the parking lot.

"Look, Ashley!" I said as a few drops of rain splashed on my nose. "There's the brown and white mini-van. I bet the Bailey Brothers were *all* in the car."

"They must have been speeding because they were so late for their show," Ashley replied.

We hurried into the theater. Glitter was still singing on stage. Where were the Bailey Brothers? Maybe they were getting changed, I thought.

Ashley, Clue and I headed backstage. We

saw Daryl and Jack standing on the side of the stage. They were watching Simon and the Shooting Stars sing.

"Hi guys," I said. "Have you seen the Bailey Brothers?"

"Yeah—they're in the instrument room. They're going on stage in a few minutes," Daryl said.

"So do you know where they were all this time?" Ashley asked them.

"Yeah—Bobby told us all about it a few minutes ago," Daryl said. "They were at Joe's Pizza—arguing for two hours!"

"Arguing for two hours? About what?" I asked. I bet it had something to do with the argument I overheard! I thought.

"Kyle told Theo he wanted to quit the group," Daryl told me. "He said he was sick of all the problems the band was having. And Bobby said he should quit, too—so he could spend more time working on his fastball."

Oh no! Were the Bailey Brothers going to

break up? They couldn't! They were the best rock band in the world!

And we hadn't caught the culprit yet! Did Theo think Ashley and I let him down?

I felt terrible. But then Jack said, "Theo convinced them to stick with the group. Then they realized how late they were for their show. They rushed home to pick up their new performance T-shirts and came back here."

"Theo got us front row tickets for tonight's show," Daryl said. "So we're going to take our seats. See you," he added as they left.

Simon and his band finished their song and left the stage.

Annette raced onstage to the microphone. "Everyone! They're finally here!" she cried. "Put your hands together for...the Bailey Brothers!"

"Yaaaay!" The fans screamed and clapped their hands. They stomped their feet and wolf-whistled. The theater rumbled with their excitement.

Theo, Kyle, and Bobby raced past us onto the stage. The audience went wild!

The Bailey Brothers started singing.

Then *kaboooooooooooooooooom*!

All of a sudden, sparks started flying out of Kyle's guitar!

Kyle dropped his guitar. It fell to the floor with a crash. "That's it! I'm out of here," he yelled. "This is getting too dangerous!"

Kyle rushed off the stage and headed for the dressing rooms. Bobby chased after Kyle. Theo stopped to talk to me and Ashley.

"Now Kyle will quit the group!" Theo shook his head sadly. "How did someone do this?" He stared at Kyle's burned guitar. "No one can get into the instrument room," he said. "I keep the door locked—and I have the only key."

"We'll check it out, Theo," I said. "You'd better go calm down Kyle." Theo nodded and left.

Annette rushed back onstage. There were a lot of boos from the audience. She told them she was sure the Bailey Brothers would be out again in a few minutes. Then she announced Glitter.

We raced to the instrument room. A shiny lock was hanging from the clasp on the door.

"Nobody could have broken through this," Ashley said, inspecting the lock.

"Then somebody must have gotten into the room another way," I said. "There must be a window, or something. Let's go outside and check it out."

As we ran out of the theater, a few heavy drops of rain hit our faces. We walked around the side of the building. "The instrument door was the third one from the exit," I said. "So, if there's a window..."

"It should be the third window from the exit," Ashley finished. "And there it is!"

Sure enough, a narrow window faced out onto the rain-drenched garden surrounding the theater. "Look!" Ashley cried. She pointed at the ground. "See those four holes in the dirt? It looks like someone put a stepladder right under this window."

"You're right!" I said. I bent down to look at the mud. "And here's something else. It looks like a footprint!"

Ashley nodded her head. "It *is* a footprint! I'd better make a sketch of it—before the rain washes it completely away!" Ashley pulled out her notebook and started sketching the footprint. "Isn't there something odd about the footprint?" she asked.

"I see what you mean," I told her. "There's something lumpy about the shape."

"We can check out the bottom of our suspects' shoes," Ashley said. "Maybe this footprint will match!"

"And I bet the matching shoe makes a *clack-clack-clack* sound," I replied.

We looked down at the muddy footprint again. "You know, Mary-Kate," Ashley said. "There's no way Heather's little high heels made that big footprint."

"Maybe Simon's tap shoe made it," I said.

When Ashley finished her sketch, it was pouring outside. As we ran inside the theater, we could hear the Bailey Brothers playing their hit song.

"Great!" Ashley exclaimed. "The Bailey Brothers are back onstage. Theo must have calmed down Kyle."

"I wish they could make it through one performance without anything going wrong."

All of a sudden, Annette came running up to us. "Mary-Kate! Ashley!"

Annette handed me a little piece of paper. "I found this note on the floor of the Bailey Brothers' dressing room."

Annette tried to catch her breath. "Someone must have slipped it under the door! But the Bailey Brothers must not have seen it!"

I opened the piece of paper and read what it said:

*Bailey Brothers beware! Do not perform again tonight. Terrible things can happen in*

*the dark!*

Annette turned pale. "But the Bailey Brothers are already on stage!" she cried.

*THUNK!*

I heard a really loud noise.

Everything went black!

# TWINKLE, TWINKLE, LITTLE STAR

I couldn't see a thing! But I could hear the audience yelling at the top of their lungs. And right next to me I could hear a familiar thumping noise. It was the sound of Clue's tail hitting the floor while she wagged it.

Ashley and I both pulled out our penlights.

"We have to get the power back on right away!" Annette shouted. She ran toward the back of the stage, where the power switch was. Ashley and I followed.

"Mary-Kate!" Ashley cried. "I think I see

something glowing on the floor." Ashley leaned over and picked something up. "It's a little shiny white star! Just like the ones Simon and the Shooting Stars wear on their outfits."

I pulled a plastic evidence bag out of my pocket. "Put it in here," I said. "We'll have to find out exactly where Simon was when the power went out." Ashley dropped the star in the bag, and I put it in my pocket.

Annette switched the power back on. I gazed around for Clue so I could get that sock, but she had trotted off somewhere.

"The show's over for tonight." Annette frowned. "I'll see you girls tomorrow. You're on after Simon and the Shooting Stars. And"— she leaned over and whispered —"let's hope you find whoever's doing this!"

Ashley and I nodded, and Annette rushed off.

I reached into my pocket and pulled out the evidence bag with the shiny white star.

"Our latest clue points to Simon," I said.

"Let's go find him."

We didn't have to look very far. Simon raced out of his dressing room, shouting as he rushed past us. "Someone ripped a star off my costume!" he yelled. "I'm going to complain to Annette right now!"

"Do you think he's making that up?" I said to Ashley. "Or could he be telling the truth?"

"Maybe Heather told him she thinks we're detectives," she answered. "So he might be saying all that to throw us off track."

"Maybe. But maybe he *is* telling the truth. And that means someone *planted* the little star by the power box."

We had to figure it all out—and fast.

We were running out of time.

The Bailey Brothers were in real danger now!

## 12

# OUR BIG SURPRISE!

By the next night, Ashley and I had been over the information in her little notebook at least one hundred times. We'd listened to what I tape recorded. We'd looked at dozens of people's shoes in the theater.

But we still hadn't found a match. And we still hadn't solved the case.

"Let's go over our two suspects again," I said as we brushed our hair in the dressing room.

"All right," Ashley said. "First, there's

Heather, the president of the Glitter Fan Club."

"Right," I said. "She doesn't like the Bailey Brothers because they get to sing more songs than Glitter."

"Second, we have Simon, the lead singer of Simon and the Shooting Stars."

"He doesn't like the Bailey Brothers because they're the ones in the newspapers all the time. Simon thinks his own group is better.

"Right," said Ashley.

"Well, we did find Heather's glitter by the sprinklers," I said.

"And we found a star from Simon's costume by the power box," Ashley pointed out.

"But they both said someone stole those things," I said.

"If someone planted clues to make Heather and Simon look bad," Ashley said, "then that means the two of them are innocent."

"Unless they're in it *together*," I exclaimed. "They're both mad at the Bailey Brothers!"

"That's true," Ashley said. "I don't know.

Maybe we're missing something somewhere. Maybe there's somebody else around here we haven't thought of."

"Somebody else who's out to get the Bailey Brothers? But who could it be?"

Ashley looked at the clock on the wall. "The Baileys are about to go on," she said. "We'd better go watch. Maybe we can prevent another 'accident.'"

"Better yet—maybe we can catch the culprit in the act!" I said.

The two of us hurried out to the side of the stage. On the way, we passed Bobby's baseball teammates, Daryl and Jack. They were wearing their baseball uniforms. "They sure are loyal friends," I told Ashley. "They come to every concert and hang out around here all the time."

"We should interview them later," Ashley said. "Maybe they've seen something weird going on that we haven't noticed."

I spotted Sam and Patty standing on the

other side of the stage. I waved and Sam waved back. Patty was kneeling down. She was painting her toenails! And I could see she had a new crown.

The Bailey Brothers played the opening notes of their hit song, "I Just Wanna Be Your Friend." The audience was clapping like crazy. Bobby and his brothers were dancing to their own music.

But what was that poking out onto the stage from behind the curtain?

Uh-oh! It was a hand!

"Ashley!" I whispered. "Somebody is reaching out a hand from behind the cur tain!"

I craned my neck to see better. The hand was reaching for the equalizer behind Kyle. The equalizer controlled the volume of the instruments.

"Oh, no!" I gasped.

Ashley and I couldn't believe it.

"Look, Ashley!" I cried. "The hand is about

to turn up the volume really loud. With those huge speakers, that could really hurt everyone's ears!"

"Come on!" Ashley yelled. "Let's catch the culprit!"

We charged backstage. It was so dark! I couldn't see anything!

*Clack-clack-clack. Clack-clack-clack!*

Suddenly I thought I saw a flash of white dart around the corner.

"Ashley! He heard us coming! He's running away!"

We raced around the corner. It was the same dark, shadowy hallway I hid in yesterday.

He was right in front of us!

"We have to tackle him!" I shouted. "Let's dive for his legs!"

We both threw ourselves at the bad guy.

"Ugh!" I grunted as I hit the floor. "I missed!"

"Ohhhh!" Ashley yelled as she slid forward

with her arms outstretched in front of her. "I almost had him!"

*Clack-clack-clack. Clack-clack-clack!*

We both heard the footsteps. "He got away again," I moaned.

"*They* got away again, Mary-Kate," Ashley told me. "I definitely felt and heard *two* different pairs of feet! The person out to get the Bailey Brothers is two people!"

# 13

# WHAT GOES UP...

**C**lack-clack-clack!

"The footsteps!" I yelled. "They're climbing the ladder to the rafters!"

"Let's go after them!" Ashley exclaimed.

We hurried to the ladder. But whoever was climbing up it had already reached the top.

"They must be hiding up there." I pointed to the rafters.

"You're right...oof!" Ashley waved her arms wildly. Then she lost her balance and tripped over something near the bottom of the ladder.

I tripped over Ashley. Soon the two of us were lying in a tangled heap on the floor.

"What happened?" I asked in confusion.

"Woof!" Clue gave me a sloppy lick on the cheek.

"I tripped over Clue," Ashley said. "She was lying right beside the ladder."

Clue was still chewing the sock from Theo's bass. "Clue—give me that disgusting, smelly sock this second!" I said.

Clue dropped the sock right in my lap. Then she put her two front paws on the ladder's rungs.

I picked up the sock with one hand and held my nose with the other. It smelled horrible! I held out the sock in front of me. Something about it looked familiar.

"Ashley," I said slowly. "Didn't we see somebody wearing blue and white socks just like this?"

Ashley blinked. Then she smiled. "We sure did," she said. "Just a few minutes ago."

"The sock Clue pulled out of Theo's bass *was* a major clue!" I cried.

"And Clue was trying to tell us that all along!" Ashley said.

"We had a lot of clues—and now they all make sense!" I said. "The clack-clack-clack footsteps and the flashes of white."

We grinned at each other.

We knew who was out to get the Bailey Brothers!

We still didn't know *why*, but we were about to find out!

# THE MOTIVE!

"**L**et's not go up there just yet," I said. "We'll make too much noise and ruin the show."

"They'll have to come down sooner or later," Ashley pointed out. "This ladder is the only way down."

"I'm going to get Sam and Patty!" I said. "Why don't you get Annette?" I told Ashley.

"Clue, you guard the ladder till we get back!" Ashley said.

Clue wagged her tail. Ashley and I both ran

in opposite directions. A minute later, we had Annette, Sam, and Patty waiting at the bottom of the ladder.

"Well? Why did you drag us over here to look at this boring ladder? If my toenail polish smudges, I'm—"

"Shhh, Patty!" I whispered. "I think I hear their footsteps now."

"Whose foot—" Patty started to say.

Sure enough, we heard feet tiptoeing down the ladder. Quiet tiptoeing, but we could still hear the *clack-clack-clack*-sound.

We all gazed up the ladder.

"Daryl...and Jack!" Patty screamed when she saw who was coming down the ladder.

Daryl and Jack were both wearing their baseball uniforms—with blue and white tube socks...and *clack-clack-clack* sounding baseball cleats!

Just then, the Bailey Brothers finished their song. The audience clapped and screamed. Theo, Bobby, and Kyle bowed, waved, and walked off the stage.

"Daryl and Jack?" Bobby asked when he saw his teammates climbing down the ladder. "What were you two doing up there?"

Ashley pointed at his friends. "Meet the rock and roll culprits," she told him.

Theo Bailey grinned at us. "I knew you two detectives would figure it out. Am I ever glad I hired you!"

Daryl glared at Jack. "I told you they were those detective twins! But you didn't believe me!" Daryl said. "That's why they didn't get scared when we tried to flood them out of the concert! They're *real* detectives!"

Jack looked embarrassed. "Sorry about drenching your band," he told us. "I guess you figured out that we planted Heather's glitter and Simon's star to make them look guilty." Jack stared down at the floor.

"But why?" Bobby asked his friends. "Why would you do all this stuff to me and my brothers? You're my best friends!"

Jack's face turned friend. "We *are* your friends," he said. "That's why we wanted to ruin your rock band. So you could spend all your time working on your pitching with us. The team needs you."

"Yeah," Daryl said. "We need you to take our team all the way to the playoffs! You're the best pitcher we've ever had. And if you go on tour in other cities, then our team will be doomed!"

Bobby frowned at his friends. "You guys did a lot of nasty stuff to my brothers—and Mary-Kate and Ashley! We all could have gotten really hurt. And because of you, my brothers and I got into the worst argument of our lives! I've never heard Theo yell at Kyle like that before!"

Daryl and Jack stared down at their cleats.

"Look, you guys," Bobby said. "After that big argument, Theo and I talked. He knows I love being on the baseball team, so we're not going on tour till *after* baseball season."

Daryl and Jack glanced up at Bobby. Both of their faces were bright red. "That's great, Bobby," Jack mumbled. "We're really sorry for all the trouble we caused."

"Next time you have a problem with me, just *tell* me," Bobby said.

"Hey, Twin Trouble," Annette said, checking her clipboard. "You're on next!"

# THE BEST PRESENT!

The next day, a package arrived for me and Ashley and Clue.

"What is it, Mary-Kate?" Ashley asked. She was wearing one of the Bailey Brothers' T-shirts Theo had given us. It looked really cool.

"It's a box from Daryl and Jack," I said.

Clue was standing up on her short hind legs, barking and sniffing at the package.

I opened the box and pulled out a letter.

*Dear Mary-Kate, Ashley and Clue,*

*We're sorry for all the trouble we caused you
and everybody else at the rock concert.
We're sending a present for Clue.*

*Daryl and Jack*

Clue climbed up onto the box and stuck her nose inside. "Woof!" she barked.

"Ugh!" I said. "What's that smell?"

Clue pulled something long, white, and stinky out of the box.

"It's a whole carton of sweaty baseball socks!" Ashley laughed. "It's the best present Clue's ever gotten."

I laughed, too. "Maybe so, but she'd better keep them in the back yard!"

"I agree," Ashley said. She held her nose with one hand and picked up the box with the other. "And when I write up this case," she said, heading for the back door, "I'm giving it a new name. Instead of the Rock and Roll Mystery, I'm going to call it the *Sock* and Roll Mystery!"

*Hi from the both of us,*

How does a mummy disappear? Good question! That's what Ashley and I had to figure out. We didn't think we would find a mystery when we went to see the mummy exhibit at our local museum. But when we got there, the mummy was gone! And that's not even the whole mystery.

We heard that the mummy was cursed. And then bad things started happening at our school. Now everyone thinks the mummy put a curse on our class! Ashley and I have to prove them wrong—fast!

Want to see how it all began? Take a look at the sneak peek on the next page for The *New* Adventures of Mary-Kate & Ashley: The Case of the Missing Mummy.

See you next time!

*Love*
*Mary-Kate and Ashley*

# The Case Of The
# MISSING MUMMY

"The mummy is gone!" I screamed.

"That's impossible!" Ashley said as she stared into the mummy's empty coffin. "We saw him lying in there just five minutes ago!"

I shivered. Ashley and I were on an overnight stake-out in our local museum. We *did* both see that mummy a few minutes ago. How could it disappear? I wondered.

The dark and spooky museum seemed even darker and spookier with a mummy on the loose!

"We have to find the mummy!" I told Ashley. "You check the exhibit rooms in the front of the museum. I'll check the ones in the back."

We raced out of the mummy's room. Ashley turned left. I turned right. Clue raced straight ahead.

I ran through the gemstone room. I saw rubies, emeralds and sapphires—but no mummy.

Then I checked out the dinosaur wing. Usually I loved the dinosaur exhibit. But not tonight. Not in the dark. The tyrannosaurus loomed in front of me—but I didn't see the mummy anywhere.

I raced out of the room, charged around the corner and ran right into a snarling tiger! I almost screamed. But then I realized I was in the mammal exhibit. "Whew!" I said. Then I slowly turned and gazed at the big scary life-like animals that lined the room. Their razor-sharp teeth glowed. I half expected the black bear to lunge for me at any second!

Then I noticed something leaning against the mountain lion.

What *was* that?

I held my breath and crept closer.

The mummy!

"Ashley!" I shouted. "Come quick!"

I heard Ashley's footsteps pounding down the hall. She raced into the room with Clue beside her.

Her eyes opened wide when she saw the mummy.

"The mummy!" she shrieked. "How do you think it got here?" she asked.

"I don't know," I said. "I can't figure it out."

"Let's go over what we *do* know," Ashley said.

"Okay. We're the only ones in the museum," I said. "We saw the mummy in its coffin. Then five minutes later, poof! The mummy disappeared!"

"And somehow it ended up right here— with the mountain lion!" Ashley added.

"Mary-Kate, there's no way that mummy walked here by itself!" she said.

I gulped. "Unless it really *is* cursed!"

# Rock & Roll & Read Mysteries Sweepstakes!

**1 Lucky Grand Prize Winner!**

## Win a trip to Los Angeles, California, to meet Mary-Kate and Ashley Olsen!

Grand prize includes all-expenses paid transportation and accommodations for 2 nights for one winner and one parent or guardian, a visit to an Olsen Twins' taping, and an ice-cream social with Mary-Kate and Ashley!

### 5 Lucky Second Prize Winners!
Win an exclusive *Mary-Kate & Ashley* Rock & Roll & Read Mysteries black vinyl jacket!

### Enter to win today!
Complete this form and the survey on the other side and send to:

*The New Adventures of Mary-Kate & Ashley*
Rock & Roll & Read Mysteries Sweepstakes!
c/o Scholastic Inc., 555 Broadway,
NY, NY 10012-3999

---

## *The New Adventures of Mary-Kate & Ashley*
## Rock & Roll & Read Mysteries Sweepstakes!

Name _____ Boy _____ Girl _____
(check one)

Address _____

City _____ State _____ Zip _____

Phone ( ____ ) _____ Birthdate _____ / _____ / _____

No purchase necessary to enter. Sweepstakes entries must be received before November 13, 1998.
See other side for details. ————————————————————————➤

## Rock & Roll & Read Mysteries Sweepstakes Survey!
### Tell Us What You Think!

TM & © 1998 Dualstar Entertainment Group, Inc. All rights reserved.

DUALSTAR PUBLICATIONS ･ PARACHUTE PRESS

■ **SCHOLASTIC**

# Rock & Roll & Read Mysteries Sweepstakes Survey!

What is your favorite *Mary-Kate & Ashley* mystery book?
The Case of _____

What is your favorite *Mary-Kate & Ashley* mystery video?
The Case of _____

Tell us 3 places where you would like to see the Trenchcoat Twins go on their next mystery adventure...

1. _____
2. _____
3. _____

What other mystery stories do you like to read?

_____
_____

If I had a private-eye dog like "Clue," he'd be a _____ dog, and his name would be_____

The name of my detective agency would be: _____

I like to read mysteries more than other kinds of stories because:

1. _____
2. _____
3. _____

The Trenchcoat Twins' motto is: WILL SOLVE ANY CRIME BY DINNER TIME.
My mystery agency motto would be:

_____
_____
_____

**Rock & Roll & Read Mysteries Sweepstakes**
**OFFICIAL RULES**

No Purchase Necessary. To enter, please fill out the Rock & Roll & Read Mysteries Survey or you may fill out the appropriate information on a separate sheet of paper. Be sure to include your name, complete address, and home telephone number. Mail completed entries to: Rock & Roll & Read Mysteries Sweepstakes, c/o Scholastic Inc., 555 Broadway, NYC, NY 10012-3999. All entries must be received by November 13, 1998. Scholastic not responsible for late, lost, stolen, misdirected, damaged, mutilated, postage due, incomplete or illegible entries or mail.

Contest is open to residents of the United States and Canada who currently attend grades 2-3. Employees, and members of their families living in the same household of Scholastic Inc., Parachute Properties, Dualstar Entertainment Group Inc., their respective parent, subsidiaries, brokers, distributors, dealers, retailers, affiliates, and their advertising, promotion and production agencies, are not eligible to enter. Sweepstakes is void where prohibited by law.

One entry per person. All entries will become the property of Scholastic Inc. and will not be returned. By entering, entrants agree to abide by these rules, warrant and represent that their entry is original work and grant to Scholastic, Parachute and Dualstar the right to edit, publish, promote and otherwise use their entries without notice or compensation.

One (1) Grand Prize Winner and Five (5) Second Prize Winners will be selected. Winners will be notified on or before November 30, 1998. Winners will be selected at random. All decisions will be final.

The Grand Prize Winner will receive an all-expenses paid two-night trip for two to Los Angeles, California. This includes airfare, ground transportation, accommodations, meals, visit to Olsen Twins' taping, and an ice-cream social with the Olsens. (Approximate retail value $4,000.00.) The five (5) Second Place winners will receive a *Mary-Kate & Ashley* Rock & Roll & Read Mysteries black vinyl jacket. (Approximate retail value $60.00.) All entrants, as a condition of entry, agree to release Scholastic Inc., Parachute Properties, Dualstar Entertainment Group, Inc., affiliates and related companies and their respective officers, directors, agents and employees, their affiliates, subsidiaries, distributors and agencies from any and all liability for injuries or damages of any kind sustained through participation in this sweepstakes and/or use of a prize once accepted.

No cash substitutions, transfers or assignments of prizes allowed, except by Scholastic in case of unavailability, in which case a prize of equal or greater value will be awarded.

Each winner will be required to sign and return an affidavit of eligibility and liability/publicity release within fifteen (15) days of notification attempt or prize will be forfeited and awarded to an alternate winner. By accepting the prize, each winner grants to Sponsor the right to use his or her name, likeness, hometown, biographical information, and entry for purposes of advertising and promotion without further notice or compensation, except where prohibited by law. Taxes on prizes are the sole responsibility of the prize winners.

For the names of the prize winners (available after December 11, 1998), send a self-addressed stamped envelope to: Rock & Roll & Read Mysteries Sweepstakes Winner's List, Scholastic Inc., 555 Broadway, New York, NY 10012-3999.

™ & © 1998 Dualstar Entertainment Group, Inc. Dualstar Video and all logos, character names, and other likenesses thereof are trademarks of Dualstar Entertainment Group, Inc. All rights reserved.

## The Adventures of MARY-KATE & ASHLEY™

**Look for the best-selling detective home video episodes.**

The Case Of The Volcano Adventure™

The Case Of The U.S. Navy Mystery™

The Case Of The Hotel Who•Done•It™

The Case Of The Shark Encounter™

The Case Of The U.S. Space Camp® Mission™

The Case Of The Fun House Mystery™

The Case Of The Christmas Caper™

The Case Of The Sea World® Adventure™

The Case Of The Mystery Cruise™

The Case Of The Logical i Ranch™

The Case Of Thorn Mansion™

**Join the fun!**

You're Invited To Mary-Kate & Ashley's™ Camp Out Party™ NEW

You're Invited To Mary-Kate & Ashley's™ Ballet Party™ NEW

You're Invited To Mary-Kate & Ashley's™ Birthday Party™

You're Invited To Mary-Kate & Ashley's™ Christmas Party™

You're Invited To Mary-Kate & Ashley's™ Sleepover Party™

You're Invited To Mary-Kate & Ashley's™ Hawaiian Beach Party™

**And also available:**

Mary-Kate and Ashley Olsen: Our Music Video™

Mary-Kate and Ashley Olsen: Our First Video™

**DUALSTAR VIDEO**

TM & ©1998 Dualstar Entertainment Group, Inc.
Distributed by KidVision, a division of Warner Vision Entertainment. All rights reserved.
A Warner Music Group Company

# Mary-Kate & Ashley
## Ready for Fun and Adventure? Read All Our Books!

## THE NEW ADVENTURES OF MARY-KATE & ASHLEY™

ORIGINAL MYSTERIES!

| | | |
|---|---|---|
| ❑ BBO29542-X | The Case of the Ballet Bandit | $3.99 |
| ❑ BBO29307-9 | The Case of the 202 Clues | $3.99 |
| ❑ BBO29305-5 | The Case of the Blue-Ribbon Horse | $3.99 |
| ❑ BBO29397-4 | The Case of the Haunted Camp | $3.99 |
| ❑ BBO29401-6 | The Case of the Wild Wolf River | $3.99 |
| ❑ BBO29402-4 | The Case of the Rock & Roll Mystery | $3.99 |

## THE ADVENTURES OF MARY-KATE & ASHLEY™

VIDEO TIE-INS!

| | | |
|---|---|---|
| ❑ BBO86369-X | The Case of the Sea World™ Adventure | $3.99 |
| ❑ BBO86370-3 | The Case of the Mystery Cruise | $3.99 |
| ❑ BBO86231-6 | The Case of the Funhouse Mystery | $3.99 |
| ❑ BBO88008-X | The Case of the U.S. Space Camp™ Mission | $3.99 |
| ❑ BBO88009-8 | The Case of the Christmas Caper | $3.99 |
| ❑ BBO88010-1 | The Case of the Shark Encounter | $3.99 |
| ❑ BBO88013-6 | The Case of the Hotel Who-Done-It | $3.99 |
| ❑ BBO88014-4 | The Case of the Volcano Mystery | $3.99 |
| ❑ BBO88015-2 | The Case of the U.S. Navy Adventure | $3.99 |
| ❑ BBO88016-0 | The Case of Thorn Mansion | $3.99 |

## YOU'RE INVITED TO MARY-KATE & ASHLEY'S™

KEEPSAKE BOOKS!

| | | |
|---|---|---|
| ❑ BBO76958-8 | You're Invited to Mary-Kate & Ashley's Christmas Party | $12.95 |
| ❑ BBO88012-8 | You're Invited to Mary-Kate & Ashley's Hawaiian Beach Party | $12.95 |
| ❑ BBO88007-1 | You're Invited to Mary-Kate & Ashley's Sleepover Party | $12.95 |
| ❑ BBO22593-6 | You're Invited to Mary-Kate & Ashley's Birthday Party | $12.95 |

- - - - - - - - - - - - - - - - - - - - - - - - - - - - - - - - - - - - -

### Available wherever you buy books, or use this order form
SCHOLASTIC INC., P.O. Box 7502, 2931 East McCarty Street, Jefferson City, MO 65102

Please send me the books I have checked above. I am enclosing $_____ (please add $2.00 to cover shipping and handling). Send check or money order—no cash or C.O.D.s please.

Name _____

Address_____

City_____State/Zip_____

Please allow four to six weeks for delivery. Offer good in the U.S.A. only. Sorry, mail orders are not available to residents of Canada. Prices subject to change.

Copyright © 1998 Dualstar Entertainment Group, Inc. All rights reserved. The New Adventures of Mary-Kate & Ashley, The Adventures of Mary-Kate & Ashley, Mary-Kate + Ashley's Fan Club, Clue and all other logos, character names, and other distinctive likenesses thereof are the trademarks of Dualstar Entertainment Group, Inc.

It doesn't matter if you live around the corner...
or around the world...
If you are a fan of Mary-Kate and Ashley Olsen,
you should be a member of

# MARY-KATE + ASHLEY'S FUN CLUB™

Here's what you get:
**Our Funzine**™
An autographed color photo
Two black & white individual photos
A full size color poster
An official **Fun Club**™ membership card
A **Fun Club**™ school folder
Two special **Fun Club**™ surprises
A holiday card
**Fun Club**™ collectibles catalog
Plus a **Fun Club**™ box to keep everything in

To join Mary-Kate + Ashley's Fun Club™, fill out the form
below and send it along with

U.S. Residents – $17.00
Canadian Residents – $22 U.S. Funds
International Residents – $27 U.S. Funds

**MARY-KATE + ASHLEY'S FUN CLUB**™
**859 HOLLYWOOD WAY, SUITE 275**
**BURBANK, CA 91505**

NAME:_____

ADDRESS:_____

CITY:_____STATE:_____ZIP:_____

PHONE: (___) _____BIRTHDATE:_____

TM & © 1997 Dualstar Entertainment Group, Inc.